To: ______________________________

From: ______________________________

ISBN: 978-1734-1509-3-3
Published in the United States by Freebody Press
www.FreebodyPress.com

Cover illustration by Samara Anjelae
Book and cover design by Carolyn Austin
Illustrations by Martha-Elizabeth Ferguson

ANGELS BEFORE YOU

A Tale of a Great Flame
following a Little Light

SAMARA ANJELAE

Table of Contents

Preface

I am, and always have been, a Soul of Little Light. A soul trying to make sense of this voyage we sail. A journey of joys and sorrows, polarities, and paradox. Somewhere on the path of life, we hear that unnamed longing in our heart. It often begins with a sick and troubled soul. In this vacuum of despair, we journey into the Night of God, the inward pilgrimage into that bubbling, bleeding heart. We find here the mysterious force that feeds our hunger, our creative potential moving us toward the light. Sometimes, it comes quickly like the wingbeats of a hummingbird, and sometimes it is slow, like a mist seeping into our consciousness over the course of a lifetime.

Once when I was lingering in the sea of grief, I was given a vision. I *saw* a flame glowing inside a golden palace. Seven colorful angel sparks danced in harmony. I *felt* fire in my heart, I *heard* a message, and I *knew* the gift of God. Yet, the burst of understanding lasted only as long as the vision. I was more lost than ever before. But to lose our way, is to arrive.

After the ecstasy came the storm. The more I rowed, the higher the waves became, until, finally, I could row no more. The storm disappeared and it became strangely quiet. On a night when stars were sleeping, I asked the Almighty Creator, whom I know by the name of God, just who am I, and what do you want of me? That night I dreamed of the ocean. The seafoam of the waves spelled out letters on the clear blue sea—live, love, and write. So, I picked up the oars, and with the help of the Silent Watchers, I expanded on my vision and wrote *Angels Before You, A Tale of a Great Flame following a Little Light*. It is more than a spiritual tale; it is also a guide for spiritual achievement for those who desire more.

I wrote *Angels Before You* over three decades ago, and it is just now finding its way to publication. Angels, your heart sparks and your lifeline to God, are timeless.

Faithfully,
Samara Anjelae

iv

The Angel Spark Tale

Long, long ago, yet somehow not so very long, there lived a glorious wise spark in the Land of Light who was known as GREAT FLAME - the Beginning of all Sparks. The guardians of the four directions soon came – Gabriel, the Angel of Water in the North; Uriel, the Angel of Earth in the South; Raphael, the Angel of Air in the West; and Michael, the Angel of Fire in the East. The Silent Watchers.

One day it was time for LITTLE LIGHT, a smaller version of GREAT FLAME, to leave home and sail into the Ocean of Wisdom, as all vessels must do. Before departure, knowing the journey would present many challenges, GREAT FLAME placed in the heart of LITTLE LIGHT a lifeline - seven ANGEL SPARKS of Truth. Upon the discovery and master-ship of these truths, the brilliance of each ray would blaze a path for her vessel to return home with light, love and wisdom.

LITTLE LIGHT's journey started in warm and friendly waters, but she gradually drifted into the Sea of For-getfulness, causing her to lose sight of her purpose and home. Confused and fearful, LITTLE LIGHT found herself shipwrecked on a seemingly deserted island, surrounded only with the Bay of Learning.

Longing for understanding and safety,
LITTLE LIGHT went searching for her lifeline.

LITTLE LIGHT discovered a sacred treasure -
a sheaf of cracked papyrus sheets.

Dear Soul,

Each of our seven sparks, tiny as they may be, possesses the splendor to grow into a beautiful and powerful flame. Our rays - Angel Sparks of Truth - are your guides on the path to gold.

Our light may seem hidden early on, but as you grow in wisdom you will learn to master each Angel Spark, making the light far and wide. If you choose not to recognize or honor us, our beams will fade, our strength will fade, and your voyage will be a dark and treacherous one, but we will never leave you. Along the journey, wavemakers will try to destroy or tear us down. But remember, you have been given sacred instruments with which you have the power to conquer these waves of darkness - a principle and a prayer to live by. Though the trials might be difficult, the rewards are great. Upon mastering an Angel Spark, through the power of love, you will receive a divine gift. In time it will not be enough just to own the gift, for you will want to share it with others.

Soul, Luminous Thread of Splendors, we are your living flame - our rays illuminate, protect, bless, and bring you to perfection. Know you never travel alone. Go forth and search until you have woven an Eternal Fire of Love. You shall return and darkness shall be no more.

- The Angels Before You

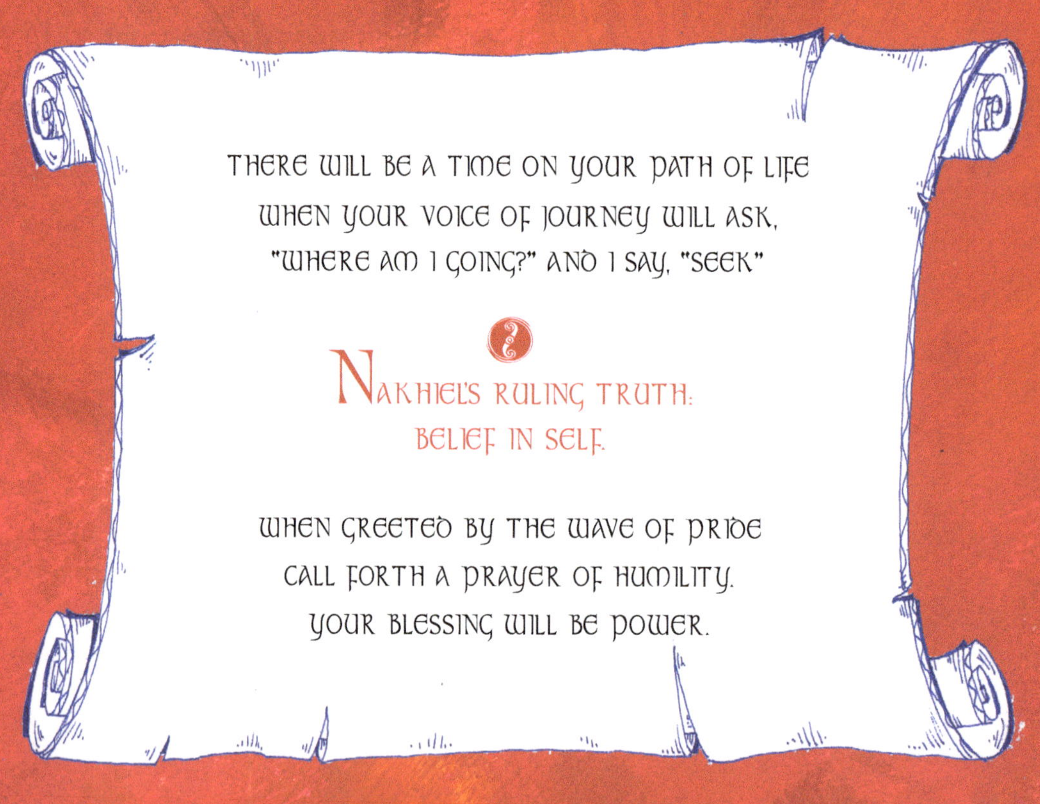

THERE WILL BE A TIME ON YOUR PATH OF LIFE
WHEN YOUR VOICE OF JOURNEY WILL ASK,
"WHERE AM I GOING?" AND I SAY, "SEEK"

NAKHIEL'S RULING TRUTH:
BELIEF IN SELF.

WHEN GREETED BY THE WAVE OF PRIDE
CALL FORTH A PRAYER OF HUMILITY.
YOUR BLESSING WILL BE POWER.

One day Salilus, the chosen soul of Little Light, started his quest on the Path of Life. He traveled many miles for the great privilege of entering the Temple of Seven Provinces.

It was well known that the temple, a fountainhead of all faiths, was a source of deep truth used for healing and understanding. This sacred place was encoded with the enduring wisdom of the ancients. Saints, teachers, and seers made pilgrimages, from time to time, to impart their blessings and share the patterns of divine insight. Upon entering, Salilus nodded respectfully to the temple aides and began to speak.

My soul is stirring, awakening, and I've come for answers.
Oh Holy Ones, where do ye see my journey going?

Brother Fire, one of the aides and light bearers, silently guided Salilus through the Majestic Hall of Learning. The students who earned their seats in this great hall were privy to the laws of heaven as told by the old masters. These masters were spirits of the celestial realm, armed with counsel, intelligence, and attention. They came to impart their wisdom in all creative forms - music, writing, painting, dancing. Brother Fire, with his rod of ruby flame, led Salilus on to a golden arched door. Brother Fire then disappeared into one of many chambers. Salilus, left alone at the door, asked himself:

Where hangs the key?
And the answer came:

The key lies in the heart.

The gate flew open. The Heart Spoke:

"Listen, O Pilgrim. I am Nakhiel, the Angel Spark of will and power. I am the birthplace of divine ideas. Let my fire blaze forth and unite with the other sparks who hang from this dim web. BELIEF IN SELF is my dynamic principle. It gives me the power to flood my crimson rays with creative expression. I am the searchlight for your vision of purpose. Watch closely the weight of your words. Excessive esteem is the work of Helel, my dark brother, who loosens the golden thread of truth. He is the selfish destroyer who wears the hood of fear, which hides his face from others.

"If you let his finger of impurity influence, you will be enticed to the Left-Hand Path where the dark forces reside. The way back to the middle is long and arduous. To ensure you will not be led astray into this land of distance, seek a sacred place of worship and pray to the Giver of all Life. The beam of my eye is whitest and purest when shielded from the lower works of Helel.

"O, Hear me now, tune to the higher key and let my power be felt! When I am neglected, I become blind and lack direction, a thread of vibration drifting without form. In order to rise in the higher heavens you must weave a garment of brightness by the power of your creative will. Let your thoughts and actions act as the loom, creating flowers of many colors. Only in time will you gain awareness and master my principle through the intensity of love. The flames of darkness will be dissolved and your journey will be purified. Your garment will shine with great splendor, reflecting your fruits of visualization. You shall have the Finger of God - the Touch of POWER. You will become a Warrior of Truth and a Beacon of Goodness for others to emulate and follow."

Nakhiel, the Ruling Angel Spark

Brother Fire, carrying his rod of ruby flame, slowly escorted Salilus from Nakhiel's chamber, leaving him with these words to ponder:

The secret is not to gain knowledge and to know, but to become.

Salilus, with rapid foot, left the temple in the direction of the path of becoming.

PRAISED BE MY LORD, BY MEANS OF ALL YOUR CREATURES, AND MOST ESPECIALLY BY SIR BROTHER SUN, WHO MAKES THE DAY AND ILLUMINES US BY HIS LIGHT. FOR HE IS BEAUTIFUL AND RADIANT WITH GREAT SPLENDOR; AND IS A SYMBOL OF YOU, GOD MOST HIGH.

PRAISED BE MY LORD, BY MEANS OF SISTER MOON AND ALL THE STARS: FOR IN HEAVEN YOU HAVE PLACED THEM, CLEAR, PRECIOUS, AND FAIR.

PRAISED BE MY LORD, BY MEANS OF BROTHER WIND, AND BY MEANS OF THE AIR, THE CLOUDS, AND THE CLEAR SKY AND EVERY KIND OF WEATHER, THROUGH WHICH YOU GIVE YOUR CREATURES NOURISHMENT.

PRAISED BE MY LORD, BY MEANS OF BROTHER FIRE, BY WHOM YOU DO ILLUMINE THE NIGHT. FOR HE IS FAIR AND GAY AND MIGHTY AND STRONG.

PRAISED BE MY LORD, BY MEANS OF OUR SISTER MOTHER EARTH, WHICH SUSTAINS US AND KEEPS US, AND BRINGS FORTH VARIED FRUITS WITH COLORED FLOWERS AND LEAVES.

– ST. FRANCIS OF ASSISI

In the second month, on the Seventh day, Soul of Little Light read the second ray:

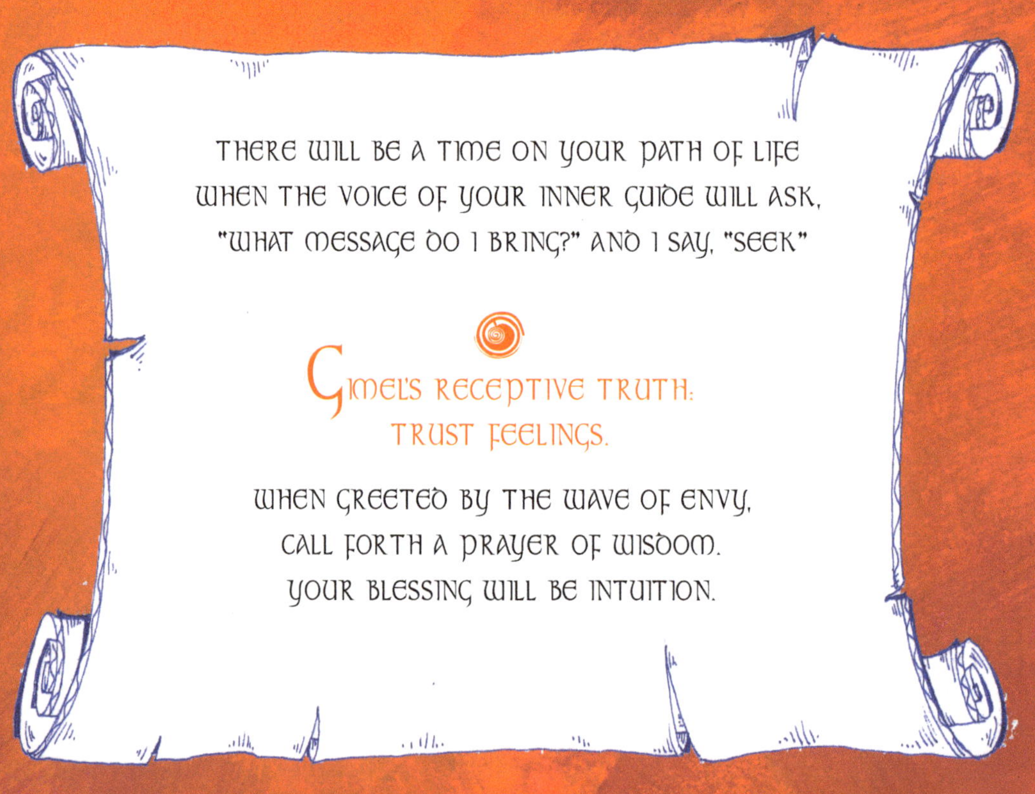
THERE WILL BE A TIME ON YOUR PATH OF LIFE
WHEN THE VOICE OF YOUR INNER GUIDE WILL ASK,
"WHAT MESSAGE DO I BRING?" AND I SAY, "SEEK"

GIMEL'S RECEPTIVE TRUTH:
TRUST FEELINGS.

WHEN GREETED BY THE WAVE OF ENVY,
CALL FORTH A PRAYER OF WISDOM.
YOUR BLESSING WILL BE INTUITION.

Salilus, with an outpouring fire of passion, ventured into the Valley of Meaningful Endeavors. The Valley's Priestess, Dweller Within, had an eye as far as the valley was wide. She felt Salilus's footsteps, heard his youthful voice, and envisioned his purse of gold many days before his arrival. In preparation for Salilus's visit,

Dweller Within left the Gate Wide Open.

Salilus descended into the valley. He saw a simple, translucent gate and felt the magnetic pull of Dweller Within. Nearby, his earthly eyes saw a more alluring gateway. As he approached the lavishly decorated door, a strange feeling came over him. Turning his ear from Dweller Within, Salilus elected to enter the more impressive gate. Once through, Salilus did not receive the festive welcome he had expected. There were no flowing vines, musical brooks, or green glades. Instead he saw ugliness and damp, cold dungeons. Salilus, wandering in darkness and confusion, cried out for help.

"Dweller Within, bring me the truth!" Salilus heard nothing. He sat in Divine Discontent. He spoke again. "Dweller Within, bring me the truth!" Salilus heard nothing. He sat in Divine Discontent. Salilus fell into the waters to cleanse his fiery emotions. Returning from the waters through the steam, he heard Dweller Within speak,

I Gave the Truth,

In a womb of envy, the ear is deaf.

The Shell Spoke:

"Hear, O Blessed One, I am Gimel, the secret place where light dwelleth. My principle, TRUST FEELINGS, is my attraction. Tap into my stream, and out of the fog comes my bittersweet essence, the true giver of wisdom. Divine Discontent is only a fear of lack. Yet, when it is not dealt with, it leads into the womb of envy, a breeding place for darkness. At the Gate of Illusion, you met my opposition, Leviathan. He is a worthless gift who attaches himself to those clothed in the coarser garments of flesh. Turn from this prince of malice who has no lighted dwelling, only a frame of fake jewels. Leviathan will continue to exist and plague you until you replenish your strength and overpower his deceitfulness. When searching for the pure knowledge and absolute truth, visit a water sanctuary. Where waters flow like living things, you will find the gift of wisdom.

"If you listen you will hear my sound. I emit tones that reveal the true temperament of an influence or situation. The inner hearing expands into a feeling, giving birth to sight and perfect understanding.

"Born from the delicate shell of my psyche is the pearl of Intuition."

Gimel, the Receptive Angel Spark

As Gimel receded to her luminous coral house, Salilus had a fleeting vision of other wayfarers traveling his same way. Dweller Within escorted Salilus out of the valley, leaving him with these words of wisdom.

Take the Higher Road of Life.
For only the pure in heart can hear.

I AM THAT SUPREME AND FIERY FORCE THAT SENDS FORTH ALL SPARKS OF LIFE. DEATH HATH NO PART IN ME, YET DO I ALLOT IT, WHEREFORE I AM GIRT ABOUT WITH WISDOM AS WITH WINGS. I AM THAT LIVING AND FIERY ESSENCE OF THE DIVINE SUBSTANCE THAT FLOWS IN THE BEAUTY OF THE FIELDS. I SHINE IN THE WATER, I BURN IN THE SUN AND THE MOON AND THE STARS. MINE IS THAT MYSTERIOUS FORCE OF THE INVISIBLE WIND. I SUSTAIN THE BREATH OF ALL LIVING. I BREATHE IN THE VERDURE AND IN THE FLOWERS, AND WHEN THE WATERS FLOW LIKE LIVING THINGS, IT IS I. I FORMED THOSE COLUMNS THAT SUPPORT THE WHOLE EARTH. . . I AM THE FORCE THAT LIES HID IN THE WINDS, FROM ME THEY TAKE THEIR SOURCE, AND AS A MAN MAY MOVE BECAUSE HE BREATHES SO DOTH A FIRE BURN BUT BY MY BLAST. ALL THESE LIVE BECAUSE I AM IN THEM AND AM OF THEIR LIFE. I AM WISDOM. MINE IS THE BLAST OF THE THUNDERED WORD BY WHICH ALL THINGS WERE MADE. I PERMEATE ALL THINGS THAT THEY MAY NOT DIE...I AM LIFE.

— HILDEGARD OF BINGEN

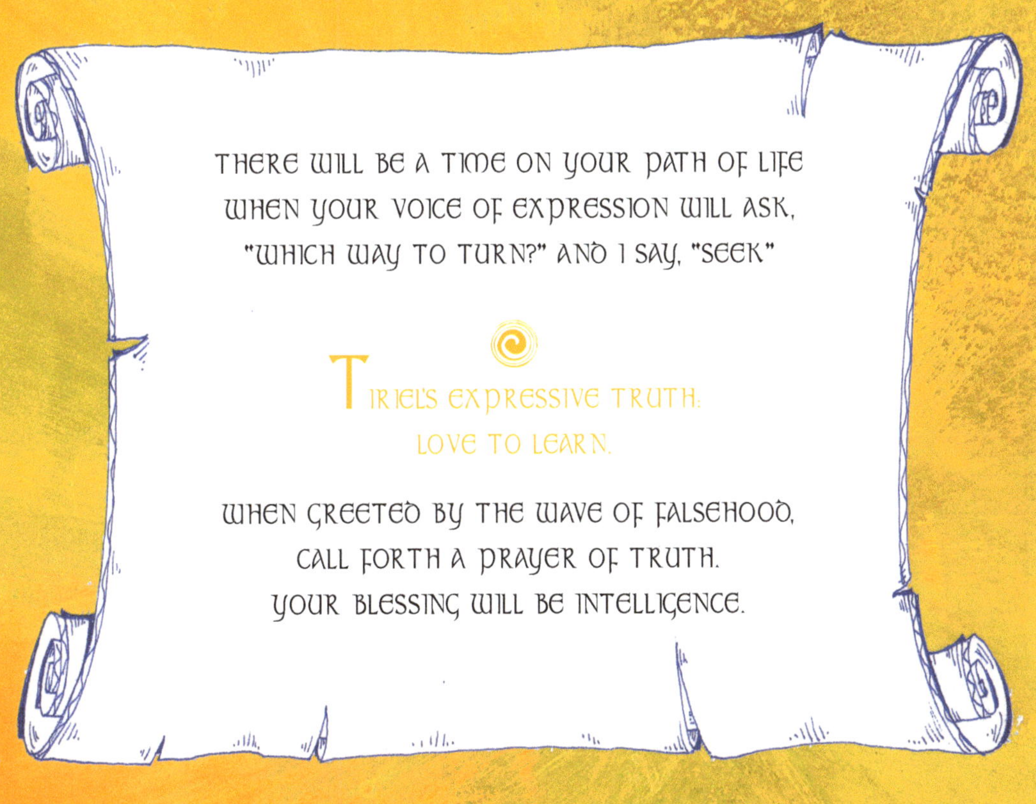
THERE WILL BE A TIME ON YOUR PATH OF LIFE
WHEN YOUR VOICE OF EXPRESSION WILL ASK,
"WHICH WAY TO TURN?" AND I SAY, "SEEK"

TIRIEL'S EXPRESSIVE TRUTH:
LOVE TO LEARN.

WHEN GREETED BY THE WAVE OF FALSEHOOD,
CALL FORTH A PRAYER OF TRUTH.
YOUR BLESSING WILL BE INTELLIGENCE.

Salilus, in no rush or hurry, and yet with no time to lose, traveled on to the Field of Opportunities. Salilus turned from right to left, and then left to right. He knew not where to go nor what to do. Salilus spoke to himself:

Amid the whirling forces, I stand confused. Which way do I express my . . .

Before completing that thought his mind had turned to Little Aspiration, a caterpillar who had crossed his path. The winds were unleashed and the sky turned dark. Salilus's head began to spin. Clouds of purple settled around him, enfolding and soothing his still form like protective wings. He found himself entwined with the caterpillar in the abyss of darkness.

Salilus and the caterpillar began to dance gently into a web of transformation. Salilus remained silent and calm within. Soon the winds were tied and the sky became clear. From the radiant sunlight a note struck upon Salilus's ear. It was unlike any sound he had heard before.

The Silver Cocoon Opened.
A Winged Messenger was born.
And a Golden Tone was heard.

The Wing Spoke:

"Hail, O Loving One, I am Tiriel, the expressive amber Angel Spark that dangles from the twist of life. Meshed between the threads of intuition and the threads of the mind, I am gifted with the woven fabric of active intelligence. LOVE OF LEARNING is my virtue. My craft is refining words and understanding the minds and hearts of all kind. Yet when caught in the net by my shadowy counterpart, Mammon, my forces are scattered to the wind like a chatter of unrecognizable tones. Mammon, a master of distorting and omitting the truth, lures the weak through mazes of destruction. He is the carrier of Falsehood, encouraging you to forget why your tiny bit of weaving is an intrinsic

part of the whole. Be silent. Learn to stand still to hear a prayer of truth. Mammon's downward-bent thoughts are intended to cause harm to others. By being silent you are protected from the snares and delusion of this prince of temptation and embraced by the scent of roses.

"When your higher learning is harmonized with underlying tones of love, a dewdrop of beauty will seep through your words and actions. Your expression will be exalted to a new height, the mount of INTELLIGENCE, echoing the Voice of God."

Tiriel, the Expressive Angel Spark

Before Salilus left the open field, Winged Messenger, with his newfound feathers of light, gave Salilus a delicate sealed topaz vase to carry his aspirations. Salilus now knew that each aspiration held a place in the greater plan, no matter how infantile or undeveloped it may be. He pressed on, chanting verse that only one of a like mind would recognize.

LORD!

WHERE WAS I?

OH YES! THIS FLOWER, THIS SUN,

THANK YOU! YOUR WORLD IS BEAUTIFUL!

THIS SCENT OF ROSES. . .

WHERE WAS I?

A DROP OF DEW

ROLLS TO SPARKLE IN A LILY'S HEART.

I HAVE TO GO. . .

WHERE? I DO NOT KNOW!

THE WIND HAS PAINTED FANCIES

ON MY WINGS.

FANCIES. . .

WHERE WAS I?

OH YES! LORD,

I HAD SOMETHING TO TELL YOU.

AMEN.

THE PRAYER OF THE BUTTERFLY
– CARMEN BERNOS DE GASZTOLD

In the fourth month, on the Seventh day, Soul of Little Light read the fourth ray:

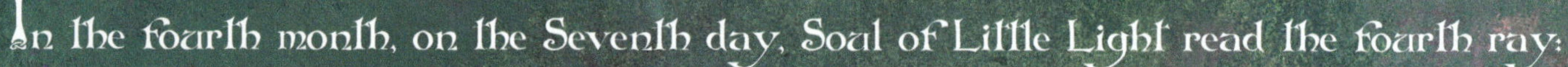

THERE WILL BE A TIME ON YOUR PATH OF LIFE
WHEN YOUR VOICE OF DESIRES WILL ASK,
"HOW DO I CONTROL?" AND I SAY, "SEEK"

HAGIEL'S EVER-FLOWING TRUTH:
BE DETERMINED.

WHEN GREETED BY THE WAVE OF GREED
AND GLUTTONY, CALL FORTH A PRAYER OF SHARING.
YOUR BLESSING WILL BE BEAUTY.

Salilus pressed his footsteps forward on the path. He began to see others ahead. He followed after them. Some moved behind. He set the pace. Receptive to his inner voice, Salilus stopped at the Garden of Spirit.

He rested his tired limbs under the soothing embrace of Sacred Tree. Seduced by the sweet maidens nearby, Salilus became lost in his pursuit of earthly delights. Days passed before he awakened from his deep unseeing stupor. Wrestling fiercely with his lower thoughts, he realized he had lost harmony with himself and had made discordant notes in his life. Traveling slowly with lagging steps, he fell into a long silence to try and hear the higher song of wholeness. Breathing slowly and deeply, he became aware of the tree guardian, Gracious One. Admiring the tree's beauty and fruit, Salilus spoke:

My soul has become sensuous, desiring great beauty and comfort.
My peaceful and fertile work is now in turmoil.
Must my desires be brought to an end?

Gracious One slipped out of her bark and opened her golden eye. Salilus, struck blind by her immortal beauty, looked toward the heavens. The All-Seeing Eye Opened. And the Veil was Lifted. Through the haze, Salilus saw the golden eye.

"O Sensuous One, I am Hagiel, the ever-flowing ray striving for infinite calm. BE DETERMINED is my sacred principle. When you have clear eyes and pure thoughts, you have the ability to create your every heart's desire. Perfect the gift to feel and see the God in all life and the rewards will be generous. Your hunger for rich surroundings will be fed by the power of my emerald light.

"Pursuing pleasures to the exclusion of all else ultimately leads you into the hands of Beelzebub, dissipating all of your creative powers and leaving you rootless. Beelzebub, my shady side, is a master of casting bitter seeds of greed and gluttony. In this manner he grows weeds of limitation and discord, entangling you in your own lower yearnings. Wither his glory by invoking a grace of sharing. Everywhere you step, sweet fragrance will come out of the ground. The giving hand replaces the greedy hand.

"When you have sensual desire, I am the light of earth. When you carry aspiration in your sealed vase, I am the light of love. When you illuminate your living by sharing your purse of gold, I am in my most beautiful form, I am the light of life. Then, and only then you shall seize God's BEAUTY."

Hagiel, the Everflowing Angel Spark

As Salilus turned his eyes backed to earth, Hagiel vanished from sight, leaving these words written in the etheric vapors:

When the eye remains open,
illumination is attained.
When the gifts are shared,
illumination is sustained.

Gracious One, now carrying a purse of gold, knew that Salilus should continue with his journey while it was still daylight. Before Salilus took his leave, Gracious One filled his pockets with gold. Enriched, Salilus left with his eye on the Star of Transcendence.

The storming of love is what is sweetest within her,
Her deepest abyss is her most beautiful form,
To lose our way in her is to arrive,
Her despairing is sureness of faith,
Her worst wounding is to become whole again,
To waste away for her is to endure,
Her hiding is to find her at all times,
To be tormented for her is to be in good health,
In her concealment she is revealed,
What she withholds, she gives,
Her finest speech is without words,
Her imprisonment is freedom,
Her most painful blow is her sweetest consolation,
Her giving is her taking away,
Her going away is her coming near,
Her deepest silence is her highest song,
Her greatest wrath is her warmest thanks,
Her greatest threatening is remaining true,
Her sadness is the healing of all sorrows.

THE PARADOXES OF LOVE ~ HADEWIJCH OF BRABANT

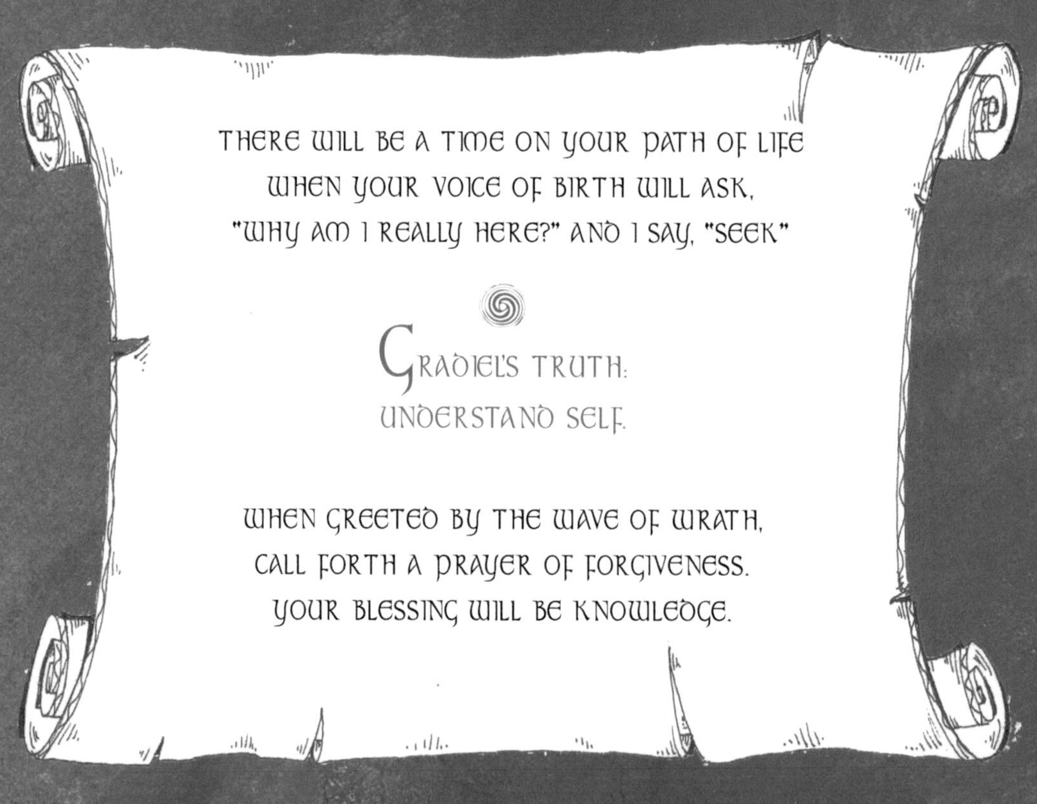
THERE WILL BE A TIME ON YOUR PATH OF LIFE
WHEN YOUR VOICE OF BIRTH WILL ASK,
"WHY AM I REALLY HERE?" AND I SAY, "SEEK"

GRADIEL'S TRUTH:
UNDERSTAND SELF.

WHEN GREETED BY THE WAVE OF WRATH,
CALL FORTH A PRAYER OF FORGIVENESS.
YOUR BLESSING WILL BE KNOWLEDGE.

The path across the far country was difficult for Salilus, yet there was no turning back. He continued with his pilgrimage. He shared his gold with others on the path and was careful not to scatter it foolishly. He was grateful for the beauty and refinement his lifted eyes could see, yet confused with the thoughtlessness and cruelty that beset his path. His fellow countrymen were inflicting pain upon each other and creating acts of moral evil. Their vision, impaired by false teachings, caused them to behave as monsters and beasts. Salilus reached out to help his brothers who had turned their face from God, but was ridiculed for his efforts. He heard the thunderbolt of vengeance and began to question his own spirit.

His sinking heart was diminishing to a dying flame. Salilus was becoming hungry for stillness and aching to climb into a secret hollow to escape his growing pain. He came upon an entrance into a cave, but to his disappointment a large round stone prevented his entry. Trying to resolve the dilemma, he focused his power on the stone. The stone guardian, Trusted Keeper, knew the cave was a place aspirants sought for refuge and enlightenment. He rose from the earth and moved aside, granting Salilus access to the cave. The opening into God's Living Temple, the Cave of Symbols, was now clear.

Trusted Keeper led Salilus to one of the chambers marked Know Thyself. Once in, Trusted Keeper bowed respectfully and slowly faded from sight. The dimly lit chamber walls were marked with strange pictures of Gods and Goddesses, hieroglyphic inscriptions, and sacred texts. Salilus ran his trembling hands over the jagged rocks, trying to make out the foreign letters and symbols. He desperately sought reasons to explain why he was born in a world of struggle and suffering. Sometimes he found what he was seeking and sometimes he failed to find any meaning. The dark hours passed. The dark days passed. He never found the key to explain all. The heat was severe and the toil was great.

In deep despair, he reached out his arms and cried out to the God he had forgotten.

I alone can do no more.
Why hast thou forsaken me?

Silence came. Standing with his arms out, Salilus formed a cross, and on that cross Salilus found his place where others have stood before him. A Revelation. Salilus had found himself. He was neither lost nor alone.

Salilus deciphered the message. The symbols were inscribed in cobalt on the wall. "Another pattern must be woven, another garment formed. Show me another weave." UNDERSTAND SELF is my principle.

🌀 Gradiel, the Seeking Angel Spark

Salilus also recognized, in the shadow, poison words of hostility, "Loosen all golden threads, and wear my garment of Wrath. Forsake all those who have forsaken you on this wasted path, Beliar."

Salilus reflected on the symbols and the meaning of Gradiel's principle. He fell to his knees. Salilus let the fire burning in his heart move him onward. His pain no longer paralyzed him. He sent forth a prayer to the Mighty Creator asking that his feelings of resentment and anger be replaced with the warmth of forgiveness before they manifested into fires of wrath. As Salilus destroyed his seeds of darkness by building thoughts worthy for a master to hear, Trusted Keeper returned to form. His many cerulean eyes appeared first, then his giving hands transmitting warmth and light. He poured a stream of energy in Salilus's hands, gracing him with strength for the rest of his upward journey. Salilus's face of tragedy and heart of sorrow were cleansed. Salilus was now emitting a sound of higher expression, and wearing God's crown of true KNOWLEDGE.

As he bade farewell, Trusted Keeper gave Salilus a lantern for casting light upon his heart. Salilus bowed gratefully and left the cave. Outside the sky was blue, and the wind blew free. The clear shine of the sun revealed the mind of God. Salilus, now with a remembered sense of direction, heard the call to completeness and took the Way of Mastery.

MAY OUR EYES REMAIN OPEN EVEN IN THE
FACE OF TRAGEDY.
MAY WE NOT BECOME DISHEARTENED.
MAY WE FIND IN THE DISSOLUTION OF OUR
APATHY AND DENIAL, THE CUP OF THE
BROKEN HEART.
MAY WE DISCOVER THE FIRE OF THE
FIRE BURNING IN THE INNER CHAMBER OF
OUR BEING — BURNING GREAT AND BRIGHT
ENOUGH TO TRANSFORM ANY POISON.
MAY WE OFFER THE POWER OF OUR
SORROW TO THE SERVICE OF SOMETHING
GREATER THAN OURSELVES.
MAY OUR GUILT NOT RISE UP TO FORM
YET ANOTHER DEFENSIVE WALL.
MAY THE SUFFERING PURIFY AND NOT
PARALYZE US.
MAY WE ENDURE, MAY SORROW BOND US
AND NOT SEPARATE US.

MAY WE REALIZE THE GREATNESS OF OUR
SORROW AND NOT RUN FROM ITS TOUCH
OR ITS FLAME.
MAY CLARITY BE OUR ALLY AND WISDOM
OUR SUPPORT.
MAY OUR WRATH BE CLEANSING, CUTTING
THROUGH THE CONFUSION OF DENIAL AND
GREED.
MAY WE NOT BE AFRAID TO SEE OR SPEAK
OUR TRUTH.
MAY THE BLEAKNESS OF THE WASTELAND
BE DISPELLED.
MAY THE SOUL'S JOURNEY BE REVEALED
AND THE TRUE HUNGER FED.
MAY WE BE FORGIVEN FOR WHAT WE HAVE
FORGOTTEN AND BLESSED WITH THE RE-
MEMBRANCE OF WHO WE REALLY ARE.

— THE TERMA COLLECTIVE

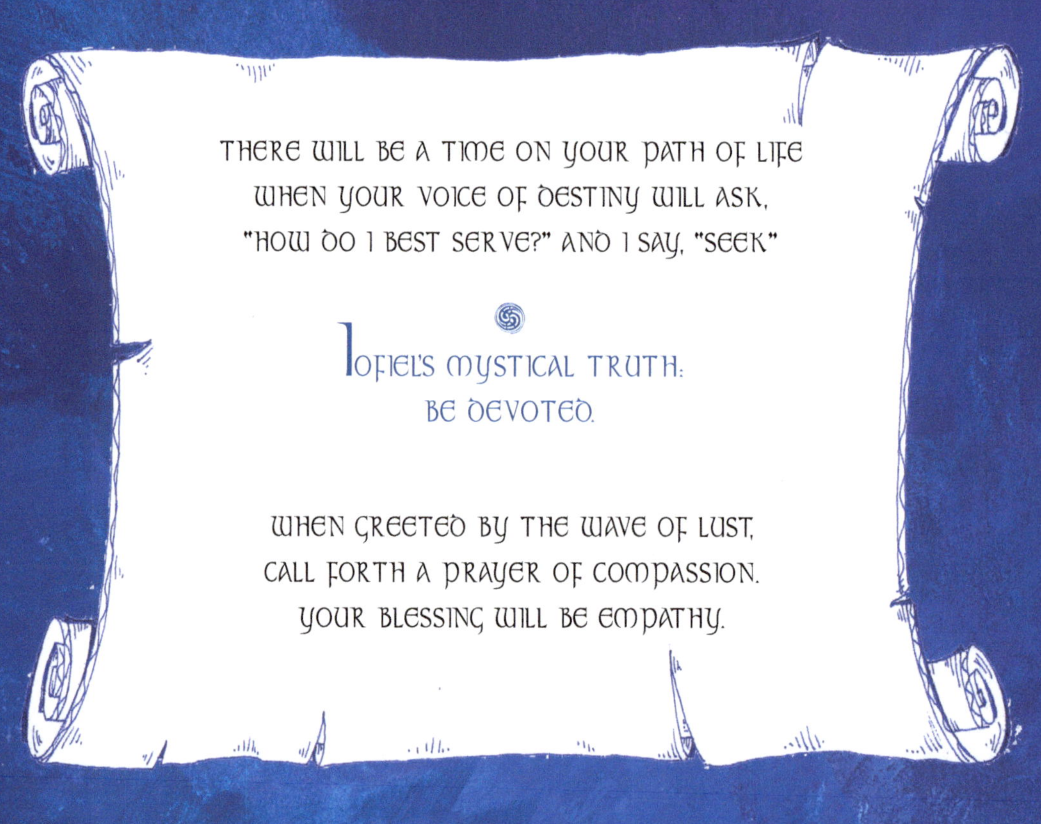

THERE WILL BE A TIME ON YOUR PATH OF LIFE
WHEN YOUR VOICE OF DESTINY WILL ASK,
"HOW DO I BEST SERVE?" AND I SAY, "SEEK"

IOFIEL'S MYSTICAL TRUTH:
BE DEVOTED.

WHEN GREETED BY THE WAVE OF LUST,
CALL FORTH A PRAYER OF COMPASSION.
YOUR BLESSING WILL BE EMPATHY.

Salilus wandered on through the wilderness of experience. His lamp cast light on the dangerous curves and treacherous pits. Other souls foolishly disappeared into the night, becoming lost in the wilderness. One day the road came to a fork, and Salilus was forced to decide which path to travel. Salilus, became deaf to his inner voice, and listened to the voice of many. He took the well-traveled road. He liked it not, for it was barren of light and fertile with chaos. Salilus became aware there was an unseen spirit walking with him, and he heard these words:

The Path that is trodden by the server is the path that ends with a blaze of glory.
It is neither the path to pleasure nor the path to pain.

Salilus closed his ear to the outer voices and honored the call of destiny. His heavy feet hurried backwards until he found a middle road, the King's Way. Traveling rapidly in strength and silence, he stumbled across the shining of a soul, Tabor, the frog. Tabor, hearing Salilus's unspoken plea for direction, called forth the rains, his frog medicine. The rains carried the powers of cleansing and healing. Salilus needed these waters to begin anew. Tabor shared with Salilus how his past solitary life, enshrined in old walls and rocks, led to his resurrection. By turning inward and spending time in deep thought, he came to know that it was by giving in service to others that his wealth would grow. And now, having carried that thought into his everyday actions, Tabor recognized as an elder of abundance and fertility. The showers began to stop and Tabor led Salilus to the Palace of Promise. He wanted Salilus to meet the Golden Flower.

Fragrant and pure, still and patient, Beloved Lotus infused the palace with the essence of opulence and beauty. Beloved Lotus invited Salilus to be a guest at her sacred center. He reclined in her white cushioned seat and began to reflect the tones of his soul. Beloved Lotus began to unfold her tiers of petals, taking Salilus first into the depths of love. Within those walls, Salilus's vision widened, and his single eye began to see past his accomplishments and into the hearts and needs of others. Then Beloved Lotus unfolded another tier of petals, taking him into the cells of sacri-

fice. Salilus's thoughts broadened and his insight quickened. In a moment of enlightenment and through the mystic dew, Salilus felt the warmth inside his heart. Faintly he heard his self say he must sacrifice the lesser to gain for the greater. Salilus reached in his sealed vase and amended his lusty aspirations, which had been only dreams of personal gain. Now, whatever he would ask for himself he would ask that also for others. And in the light, Salilus saw the light. Suddenly, he felt the presence of Iofiel, forthright and larger than life.

The Petal Spoke:

"O Destined One, I am Iofiel, the mystical Angel Spark. I am a spinner and weaver of deep desire, the divine design of the greater plan. My darts, BE DEVOTED, are my power and principle. They are like flaming arrows that fly from my indigo tapestry. When my work is done with love, I am the silken thread that manifests gifts of spirit in the kingdom of matter, serving all brethren. Stand at the center and look on every side. Let your love be an inclusive love and not a narrow love. When the last thread is strung, you will have woven a cloth of your own doing. It will serve you either as a strong coat of protection or a weak fabric of self-destruction.

"Temptations of the heart prove plentiful for those who are weak. Arm yourself against the murky entrapments of Asmodeus. He is the false prophet who dissolves into the shadow of your mind, clad in seductive attire to entrap a willing heart. Your weak spot is his gain. He who cleanses himself of selfishness and lust may have the fullest use of my riches, thus striking fear and terror in the boiling spirit of Asmodeus.

"Ask for the blessings from God as you serve your destiny. Seek the Most Holy Place and commune with the Supreme Power for guidance to your calling. Let simplicity be your spirit's compass. A prayer of warmth helps your higher self take root and blossom into perfection. As an award for your faith and loyalty to a higher purpose, you have God's promise to know the Glory of the One. You feel within yourself the joys and pains of another, a gift that transcends compassion. And you will behold the virtue of EMPATHY."

🌀 Iofiel, the Mystical Angel Spark

On the eve of departure, Salilus saw the head of days in the bosom of Beloved Lotus. Tabor showed Salilus the magical view, the perfectly formed leaves that will one day blossom into a thousand petals. Salilus, with his lower light thrown upward, was ready to serve. He saw the path to Godhood.

And there stood the mountain.

LAST NIGHT, AS I WAS SLEEPING,
I DREAMT – MARVELOUS ERROR! –
THAT A SPRING WAS BREAKING
OUT IN MY HEART.
I SAID: ALONG WHICH SECRET AQUEDUCT, OH
WATER, ARE YOU COMING TO ME, WATER OF
A NEW LIFE
THAT I HAVE NEVER DRUNK?

LAST NIGHT, AS I WAS SLEEPING,
I DREAMT – MARVELOUS ERROR!
– THAT I HAD A BEEHIVE
HERE INSIDE MY HEART.
AND THE GOLDEN BEES
WERE MAKING WHITE COMBS
AND SWEET HONEY
FROM MY OLD FAILURES.

LAST NIGHT, AS I WAS SLEEPING,
I DREAMT – MARVELOUS ERROR! –
THAT A FIERY SUN WAS GIVING
LIGHT INSIDE MY HEART.
IT WAS FIERY BECAUSE I FELT
WARMTH AS FROM A HEARTH
AND SUN BECAUSE IT GAVE LIGHT AND
BROUGHT TEARS TO MY EYES.

LAST NIGHT, AS I SLEPT,
I DREAMT – MARVELOUS ERROR!
– THAT IT WAS GOD I HAD
HERE INSIDE MY HEART.

– ANTONIO MACHADO

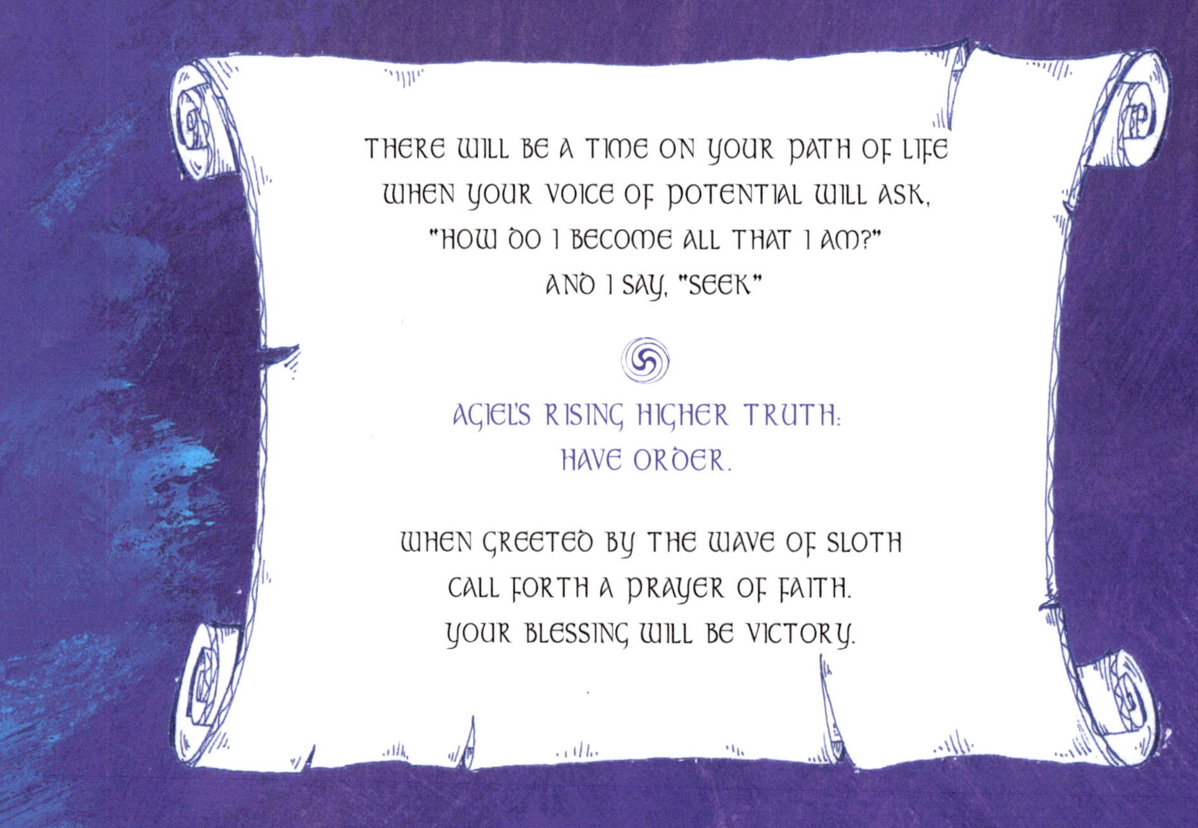

THERE WILL BE A TIME ON YOUR PATH OF LIFE
WHEN YOUR VOICE OF POTENTIAL WILL ASK,
"HOW DO I BECOME ALL THAT I AM?"
AND I SAY, "SEEK"

AGIEL'S RISING HIGHER TRUTH:
HAVE ORDER.

WHEN GREETED BY THE WAVE OF SLOTH
CALL FORTH A PRAYER OF FAITH.
YOUR BLESSING WILL BE VICTORY.

Salilus set foot on the holy ground of the Mountain of Most High. He chose to go straight up the face of the mountain. As he made the steep climb, a golden mist was beginning to appear around his head and a violet hue settled around his body. A silver eye and a golden ear opened inside a nearby waterfall. The eye watched wide as Salilus became bogged down in mud and debris. The ear listened far to Salilus's discouraging thoughts as he attempted his ascent. Lurking in Salilus's shadow was a dark figure, luring him to abandon his path and follow his shadow around the mountain.

Catching drift of Salilus's perceptions was Aaliyah, the water sprite hidden in the waterfall. Salilus heard the sound of rushing water as if it was music coming down from the heavens. Salilus was led to the waterfall by the celestial tones and the flickering lights he saw in the fringe of his vision. Distracted from the dark force, Salilus bent down to the water for a drink. Through the waters, Aaliyah's heart-shaped face and slender, ethereal body appeared to him. Her tiny hands were busy mixing the rays from the sunlight with the swirling forces of the water to create a magnetic mixture. Spraying a shower of silver droplets in all directions, Aaliyah handed Salilus a magic cup, a crystal goblet.

Partake of my Drink.
And your Cup will Flow
With the Pure Essence of Life

Salilus obeyed her command and drank from the cup. A sudden stream of life-energy poured through him. Aaliyah knew Salilus was close to finding the key to reach the summit. Aaliyah lifted the falling waters and raised a window barely enough for Salilus to see in a lighted portal.

The Waters Spoke:

"Hark to my joyous tone, O Bright Pilgrim. I am Agiel, the rising higher Angel Spark. Turn the key to my power and principle, HAVE ORDER, and reap an everlasting reward. If you find my silver cord, follow it to the end, thirty-three notches high. It will lead you back to your illuminated soul. Do not pay any attention to the muddy forces of Belphegor. He is the beast who lurks behind you, carrying the wave of sloth. His poisonous breath can creep over you like a hazy trance, encouraging you to forget your higher aspirations. Dispel his shadows of darkness and his weapon of chaos by remaining true to your greater voice. Use a prayer of faith to help sustain you in your tiresome and difficult times."

⑨ Agiel, The Rising Higher Angel Spark

The violet window began to close before Salilus could hear more from Agiel. The thunders crashed around the mountaintop as Salilus went searching for the silver cord Agiel had described. A beam of light illuminated the silver thread at the base of the mountain. He worked his way to the golden end with steady effort and discipline.

Salilus, near the highest point of the moun-tain, looked up and saw a tall figure on higher ground. He was standing between earth and heaven, clothed in a white robe with wings of flame and golden halo around his head. He was known as Eth, Ancient of Days. He had one foot on land and the other on sea. In his right hand he held a flaming sword. Behind him was the rising sun and on his  brow were the holy letters of the Creator's blessed name. Salilus spoke to Eth, Ancient of Days.

I have searched and searched for all the threads of truth.
How does one weave to your Great Height?

Eth, Ancient of Days, replied

Lo! If thou art a True seeker,
Thou shalt keep Steadfast in thy Search
and God's Laws shall be revealed
Exalting thy presence to Great Heights.

Salilus continued his journey in search for all the truths. One morning at sunrise, through his own efforts, his own will, and his own imagination he worked toward the manifestation of weaving an arch to reach the realms of Eth, Ancient of Days. As he built the bridge, he saw with his inner eye an astral status of the purity and clarity of his heart. Salilus, not completely comfortable with the status, worked even harder to reach his destination. As he became conscious of where he was making full use of his potential and where he was falling short, a record of his innate qualities flashed before him. The arch was beginning to radiate with royalty. Salilus was close to completion when enlightenment came to him. A complete visual history appeared of everything that had ever happened to him on his journey. He realized that God's Eternal Plan had always been part of his life, mind, heart, hand, eye, and ear. Salilus knew he had been wrong when he had thought earlier that God had forsaken him. By sunset Salilus had reached his goal. He had woven a rainbow arch of transcendent splendor using the power of all the sparks working together.

Eth, Ancient of Days, stepped forth with a sound of eternal harmony, and the power of the letters inscribed on his brow opened the windows of Heaven. Salilus was back at the Temple of Seven Provinces. He peered through the window and saw that there were seven chambers with candles in place, waiting to be lit. Salilus entered the temple. The temple had grown in light and beauty. Its line, walls, and decor had expanded in depth and breadth. Eth, Ancient of Days, led Salilus to the golden arched door. This time at the door, Salilus knew he was not alone.

Salilus spoke passionately to himself:

Seven Gates Flew Open.

Eth, Ancient of Days, and Salilus went through each of the provinces. They started with Nakhiel's chamber. Brother Fire was holding a balance in his hand. He weighed Salilus's actions performed during his lifetime thus far. The scarlet scales tipped up and down. Brother Fire found Salilus worthy to pass on to the next province. Salilus silently said a prayer of gratitude. At the second province, Dweller Within gave Salilus a book from Gimel. In the book was a copper mirror. Salilus peered at the glass and could see the Divine Face within himself. In Tiriel's sunny chamber, Salilus took a solemn promise under the guidance of the Winged Messenger. Contained within this oath was a secret and power that revealed Salilus's intricate part in the design of creation. Continuing on, Eth, Ancient of Days, took Salilus to

Hagiel's chamber. Gracious One gave Salilus a hazel eye amulet to ward off those who might seek to harm him. In Gradiel's province, Salilus was given a turquoise mandala by Trusted Keeper. Within it, the turning of the wheels revealed the entire workings of the cosmos. Salilus felt his awareness broaden as he went toward Iofiel's chamber. Beloved Lotus uncoiled herself like a sleeping serpent being awakened. She opened to her highest potential, a thousand-petaled lotus reflecting the brightness of Salilus's indigo aura.

Eth, Ancient of Days, and Salilus were standing at the top of the mountain. Agiel was now fully visible for Salilus. She placed an amethyst ring on his finger. It was engraved with a star. Salilus now had the power to turn this star into a ring of fire, subduing all waves of darkness.

The Heavenly Choir sang and the Voice of Trumpet began playing. All seven chambers were fully lit. A thread of radiance bringing forth God's eternal truth united them. The ceremony of order was complete. Salilus had uncoded each key buried within the Temple of Seven Provinces. Through the underlying force of Venus, Star of Love, each Angel Spark merged into a center of living light. Salilus was emitting a sound of vibration that transformed the golden mist of flame around his head into a brilliant white halo. He was clothed in a robe of luminous matter, and he bore on his back a set of radiant wings. Eth, Ancient of Days, on behalf of Agiel and the other sparks gave Salilus the inherited gift that so few know of

The Gift of Victory,
the Signature of God.

Upon Salilus's shoulder was the bird of peace, and on his feet the sandals of the messenger. Salilus in that moment spoke.

Holy of Holies,
into thy hands
I give my spirit.

Salilus stood before Eth, Ancient of Days and took his sword, releasing Eth onto a higher task. Salilus now guards the doorway between the Holy Plane and the Seven Provinces with his mighty wings and flaming sword. Salilus stands on the mountaintop. Beneath him are the valleys and the plains, the gardens and caves, the water and streams, and the clouds in the sky. Above him is the blue of heaven.

And inside him is radiance of the rising sun.

I AM ONLY A SPARK
  MAKE ME A FIRE.
I AM ONLY A STRING,
  MAKE ME A LYRE.
I AM ONLY A DROP
  MAKE ME A FOUNTAIN.
I AM ONLY AN ANT HILL
  MAKE ME A MOUNTAIN.
I AM ONLY A FEATHER
  MAKE ME A WING.
I AM ONLY A RAG,
  MAKE ME A KING!

                – AMADO NERVO

And in Divine Time, LITTLE LIGHT rows out of
the dark night, and turns inward to the Great Sea of the Waters
of Life. War breaks out between the Sparks of Light and the
Waves of Darkness.

LITTLE LIGHT saves her lifeline of seven splendors. The Silent Watchers rejoice as LITTLE LIGHT
becomes a Salilus and guides other vessels home that are caught
in the Current of Despair.

Soul of LITTLE LIGHT is now clothed with the
Fire of Love,

a GREAT FLAME,

Her Angel Self, SPARK-EL

Afterword

Angels Before You: A Tale of a Great Flame following a Little Light is a spiritual tale and guidebook that explores the pilgrimage of the soul on an inward journey to the heart. Seven short stories within the tale build on each other to introduce seven angels who symbolize the seven chakras – energy centers of the body in which they govern. Each chakra represents a different level of consciousness, ranging from the lowest for physical survival (red root chakra) to the highest for spiritual enlightenment (violet crown chakra.)

Angels Before You embodies some of the symbolic language and teachings that are found in the Bible, the Kabala, Esoteric Astrology, and Hindu philosophy. Soul of Little Light is the ageless archetype, the ever-enduring hero. The reader travels with the mythic hero as he/she undergoes trials, learns from those trials, and eventually faces and conquers death in some form before completing the journey.

The higher meaning and symbolism used in the book are inspired mainly from Helena P. Blavatsky, one of the founders of the Theosophical Society. Toward the end of the 18th century, Blavatsky shared in her writings her extensive knowledge of symbolism, metaphysics, and philosophies and religions of the world as taught to her by Tibetan teachers. The works of Alice Bailey were also used as a resource. Several volumes by Bailey delve extensively into the psychological make-up of a human being through their incarnations as an evolving spiritual entity.

In the end, Soul of Little Light saves her lifeline of seven splendors and is clothed with the Fire of Love, a Great Flame: Spark-el. Spark is defined as a glowing bit of matter. In the Talmud and Targum, sparks are said to be an order of angels. El is an old Hebrew word for God, and in many other ancient languages, it means "radiant," or "shining one." El is a common ending of the archangels and many angel names. In essence, Spark-el means we have reached our highest potential, our angel self; a glowing bit of God.

I assigned the twelve astrological signs and their ruling planets to an appropriate angel and chakra based on my knowledge and research. Each sign identifies a principle to live by, a corresponding weakness to be aware of, and a blessing (gift) that can be achieved. The seven waves of darkness in the story are descriptive of the seven deadly sins from the Bible. Each identifies with the fallen angel's name or a nickname given to them. A prayer closes each chapter and is a representation of different cultures and mystics.

Grateful acknowledgement is made to the writings from St. Francis of Assisi, Hildegard of Bingen, Carmen Bernos de Gasztold, Hadewijch of Brabant, The Terma Collective, Antonio Machado, and Amado Nervo.

Summary

Angel Spark	Nakhiel	Gimel	Tiriel	Hagiel	Gradiel	Ioficl	Agiel
Type	Ruling	Receptive	Expressive	Ever-Flowing	Seeking	Mystical	Rising Higher
Chakra	Root	Spleen	Solar Plexus	Heart	Throat	Third Eye	Crown
Planet	Sun	Moon	Mercury	Venus	Mars	Jupiter/Neptune	Saturn/Uranus
Sign	Leo	Cancer	Gemini/Virgo	Taurus/Libra	Scorpio/Aries	Sagittarius/Pisces	Capricorn/Aquarius
Voice Of	Journey	Inner Guide	Expression	Desires	Birth	Destiny	Potential
Principle	Belief in Self	Trust Feelings	Love to Learn	Be Determined	Understand Self	Be Devoted	Have Order
Wave	Pride	Envy	Falsehood	Greed/Gluttony	Wrath	Lust	Sloth
Prayer	Humility	Wisdom	Truth	Sharing	Forgiveness	Compassion	Faith
Blessing	Power	Intuition	Intelligence	Beauty	Knowledge	Empathy	Victory

Glossary of Terms

Aaliyah

A variant of the Hebrew Aliyah: to ascend. Rf. *A World of Baby Names*. Aliliyah-one of the many names of the angel Metatron. Rf. *A Dictionary of Angels*

Angel Sparks

- Nakhiel: The presiding intelligence angel of the sun, when the sun enters the sign of Leo.
- Gimel: An angel that corresponds to the Moon.
- Tiriel: The presiding intelligence angel of the planet Mercury.
- Hagiel: The presiding intelligence angel of Venus when that planet enters the signs of Taurus & Libra.
- Gradiel: The presiding intelligence angel of the planet Mars when that planet enters the signs Aries & Scorpio.
- Iofiel: The presiding intelligence angel of the planet Jupiter.
- Agiel: The presiding intelligence angel of the planet Saturn.

El

El, is an ancient Hebrew word for God. It has a common origin with many other ancient words in other languages, often meaning radiant one or shining being. Rf. *Angels: An Endangered Species*

Eth, Ancient of Days

Eth-An angelic power, a ministering angel, charged with seeing to it that all events occur at their appointed time. Eth means time. Rf. *The Zohar Miquez*. Ancient of Days-a term to denote the holy ones of the highest. The most exalted and venerable of the angels. Rf. *A Dictionary of Angels*

Salilus

Salilus is identified in magical arts as a genius who sets doors open. Apollonius of Tyana, a 1st century AD Greek philosopher, tells us in his work, *The Nuctemeron*, that Salilus is a genius angel of the 7th hour. Rf. *Levi, Transcendental Magic*. Rearrange the letters in Salilus and you have: all is us.

Sparks

Sometimes referred to as an order of angels. The sparks are sometimes included among the orders when equated with the brilliant ones or with the splendors. Rf. *A Dictionary of Angels*. These angels of grace bestow blessings from on high, usually in the form of miracles. They are most associated with heroes and with those who struggle for good. It is said that they instill courage when it is needed most. The Brilliant or Shining Ones are also known as Virtues. Rf. *Angels: An Endangered Species*. The Divine or Vital Spark is supported by all of the ancient religions, from the Vedic, to the Egyptians, from the Zoroastrian to the Jewish.

Wavemakers

According to a list complied in 1589 by a demonologist named Binsfield, the following fallen angels demons were associated with a particular evil. Rf. *The Columbia Encyclopedia, Fifth Edition*.
Lucifer - pride, Helel is another name for Lucifer. Rf. *Godwin's Cabalistic Encyclopedia*
Leviathan - envy
Mammon - avarice
Beelzebub - gluttony
Satan - anger, Beliar is another name used for Satan. Rf. *A Dictionary of Angels*
Asmodeus - lechery
Belphegor - sloth

Other Books by Samara Anjelae

Angel Girl and the Hawk (novel)

Angel Prayers

100 Ways to Attract Angels

My Guardian Angel

My Fairy Godmother

My Magical Mermaid

Wonder Windows Gift Box

SamaraAnjelae.com